IN VERMIS VERITA[S]
(A tiny tale inspired by *Registry of D[eath]*)

"It's nothing to do with mortality but it's to do with the great beauty of the color of meat." So said Francis Bacon, an artist of the twentieth century, explaining why he painted scenes of gore and squalor. While admiring his sentiment, I would also postulate that Bacon's appreciation for the color of meat made him a connoisseur of the very mortality he pretended to eschew.

I consider myself a connoisseur of mortality. While my millions of brethren and sistren chew, chew, chew their way through whatever offal comes along, inexorable but mindless, I preserve my energies for the sweetest meat: the carcass tainted by fear. The carcass that suffered the protracted death, the agonizing death. Meat crisped alive by fire, meat sliced open by steel, meat with a bullet in its gut.

Here in the slaughterhouse, I dine well.

It is everything to do with mortality. It is the great beauty of the color of meat, of its many colors: the spongy purple of drowned flesh, the translucent rose of fresh viscera, the seething indigo of rot. Bacon must have painted in the slaughterhouse. It is the great beauty of the flavor of meat, of its many flavors.

When we reduce a carcass to bone, we not only reveal its structure; we become composed of its elements. For most of the others, this is a matter of breaking down proteins and replenishing simple larval tissues. For me it is a kind of catharsis. I take on the qualities of the deceased, I am nourished by his perceptions, and perhaps somehow I aid in releasing his soul.

Consequently, I have lived thousands of lives. I have memorized countless tomes, and written more than a few. I have constructed dynasties, then torn them down or watched them fall. I have been a foetus in a womb and a guru in a cave. I have digested the concepts of "freedom" and "love" and "eternity," and excreted them, over and over again.

Men kill other men, sometimes for sport, sometimes for love, sometimes just sending them to the slaughterhouse to feed still more men—or, if left too long, to feed me and my kin. Each one thinks he has lived in the worst of times, but nothing has ever been different.

I curl in the slightly damaged brain of a young man who died for no particular reason, after a protracted and honorable hunt. The glistening whorls are dissolving, coming unglued, breaking down into their chemical components. I gorge myself on the primordial soup of his mind. The terrible realization that dawned upon him at the moment of death sharpens the taste.

I become drunk on his flood of experiences and emotions. I synthesize his knowledge. I live his entire life in the time it takes to eat a path through his liquefying brain. I wallow in his world. I die his weary death.

As always, it makes me glad to be a maggot in the slaughterhouse and not a man.

Poppy Z. Brite

New Orleans, 1996

⊗ 0731521

Printed in Canada

For a FREE catalog containing hundreds of comics, books, and other great merchandise, write to the Kitchen Sink Press address below, call 1-800-672-7862, e-mail kitchensp@aol.com, or fax 1-413-582-7116.

Library of Congress Cataloging-in-Publication Data

Coyle, Matthew
    Registry of Death / artist, Matthew Coyle : writer, Peter Lamb
                  p.   cm.
        ISBN 0-87816-448-0
       I. Lamb, Peter.   II. Title
  PN6727.L36C69   1996   96-22478
  741.5'973—dc20   CIP

Registry of Death ©1996 Matthew Coyle and Peter Lamb. In Vermis Veritas © 1996 Poppy Z. Brite. Kitchen Sink, Kitchen Sink Press, and the Kitchen Sink Press logo are registered trademarks of Kitchen Sink Press, Inc. All rights reserved. Published by Kitchen Sink Press, Inc., 320 Riverside Drive, Northampton, MA 01060. The stories, characters, and incidents portrayed in this publication are entirely fictional. No actual persons, living or dead, are intended to be depicted, but for purposes of satire, and should not be inferred. No reproduction is allowed without the consent of the publisher. First Printing: November 1996 5 4 3 2 1

ARTIST
Matt Coyle

WRITER
Peter Lamb

INTRODUCTION BY
Poppy Z. Brite

PUBLISHER
Denis Kitchen

EDITOR
Catherine Garnier

ART DIRECTOR
Amie Brockway

DESIGNER
Lisa Stone

EDITORIAL INTERN
Aaron Mulvany

SENIOR VP, PRODUCTION
Jim Kitchen

EXECUTIVE VP
Scott Hyman

CHIEF FINANCIAL OFFICER
Corey J. Schwartz

SENIOR DIRECTOR, SALES AND MARKETING
Jamie Riehle

SALES AND MARKETING ADMINISTRATOR
Christie Lauder

NATIONAL DIRECTOR OF SALES
Eric Hyman

DIRECTOR OF LEGAL AFFAIRS
Dorothy Varon

CUSTOMER SERVICE MANAGER
Karen Lowman

MANAGING EDITOR
John Wills

PROMOTIONS DESIGNER
C. Evan Metcalf

WAREHOUSE MANAGER
Vic Lisewski

REGISTRY of DEATH

BY MATT COYLE AND PETER LAMB

INTRODUCTION BY POPPY Z. BRITE

NORTHAMPTON, MASSACHUSETTS

Older people still talk of how it used to be before the Registry. But for the people of my generation a world without the Registry is beyond comprehension. According to the history books the period immediately prior to the Registry was characterized by the worst kind of liberal democratic politics, a time of communists and bleeding hearts.

I have worked for the Registry since the age of seventeen. I am a Registry Elimination Officer, my job is to execute routine warrants for the elimination of illegals—killing for a living.

Perhaps I should say that I used to work for the Registry, for things have changed and I now find myself on the other side of the system. For reasons beyond my comprehension I have suddenly become an enemy of the state. I have no long-term plan as to how to avoid elimination, and for now I must concentrate on the immediate danger.

The warrant for my elimination will be issued under the "Births, Deaths, and Marriages Reform Act" of '67, which allows the Registry to "remove" undesirable individuals from the Register. My only advantage at this time is that I know this place well. I also know my enemy well, but this is not an advantage—they may as well be me, for I once did as they now do.

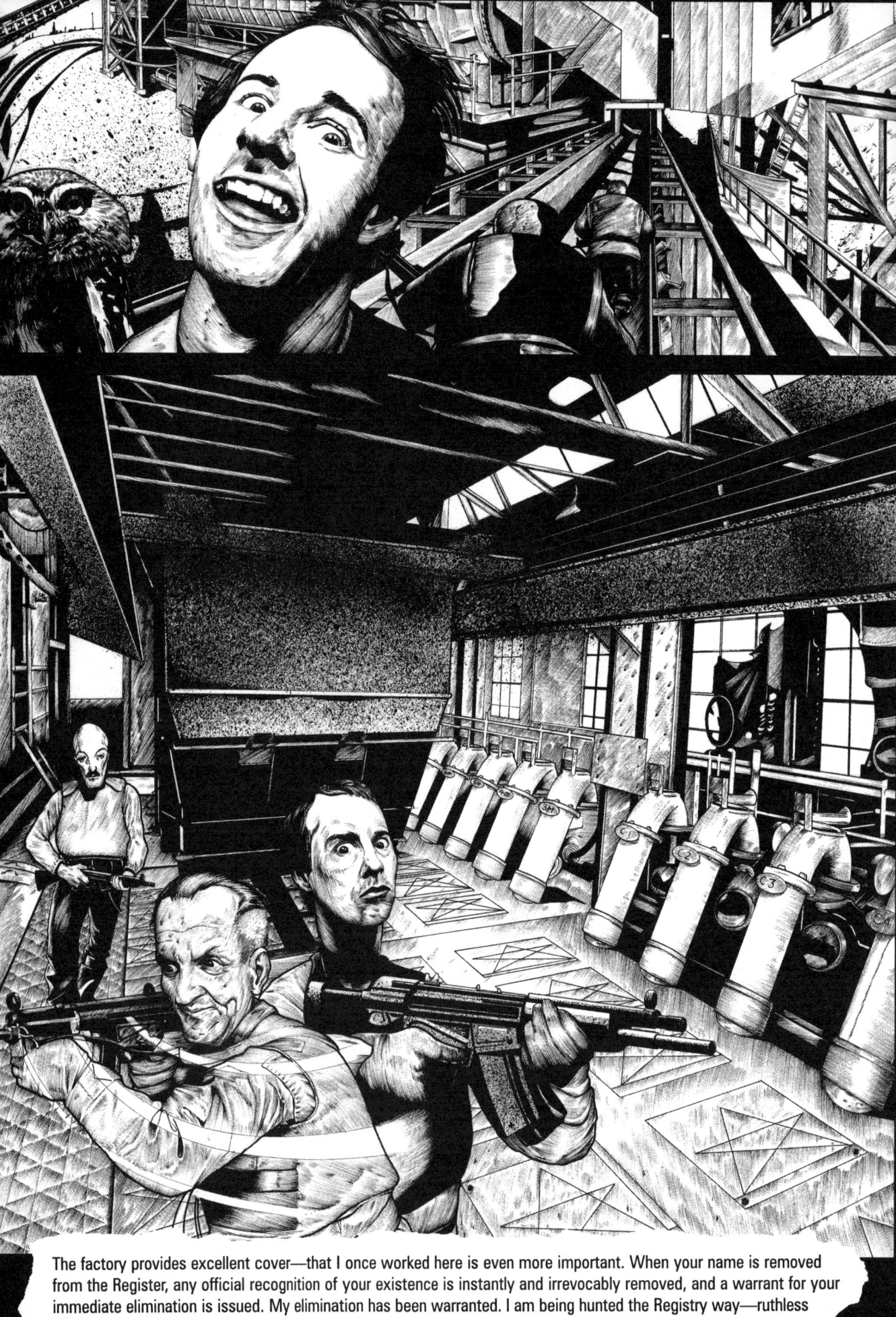

The factory provides excellent cover—that I once worked here is even more important. When your name is removed from the Register, any official recognition of your existence is instantly and irrevocably removed, and a warrant for your immediate elimination is issued. My elimination has been warranted. I am being hunted the Registry way—ruthless with just a hint of unbalanced evil, and one hundred percent effective—eventually.

I'm safe here with my gun, at least for now. The euphoria of an elimination will be coursing through their systems by now. It's difficult for me to remain in control, but I must stay calm.

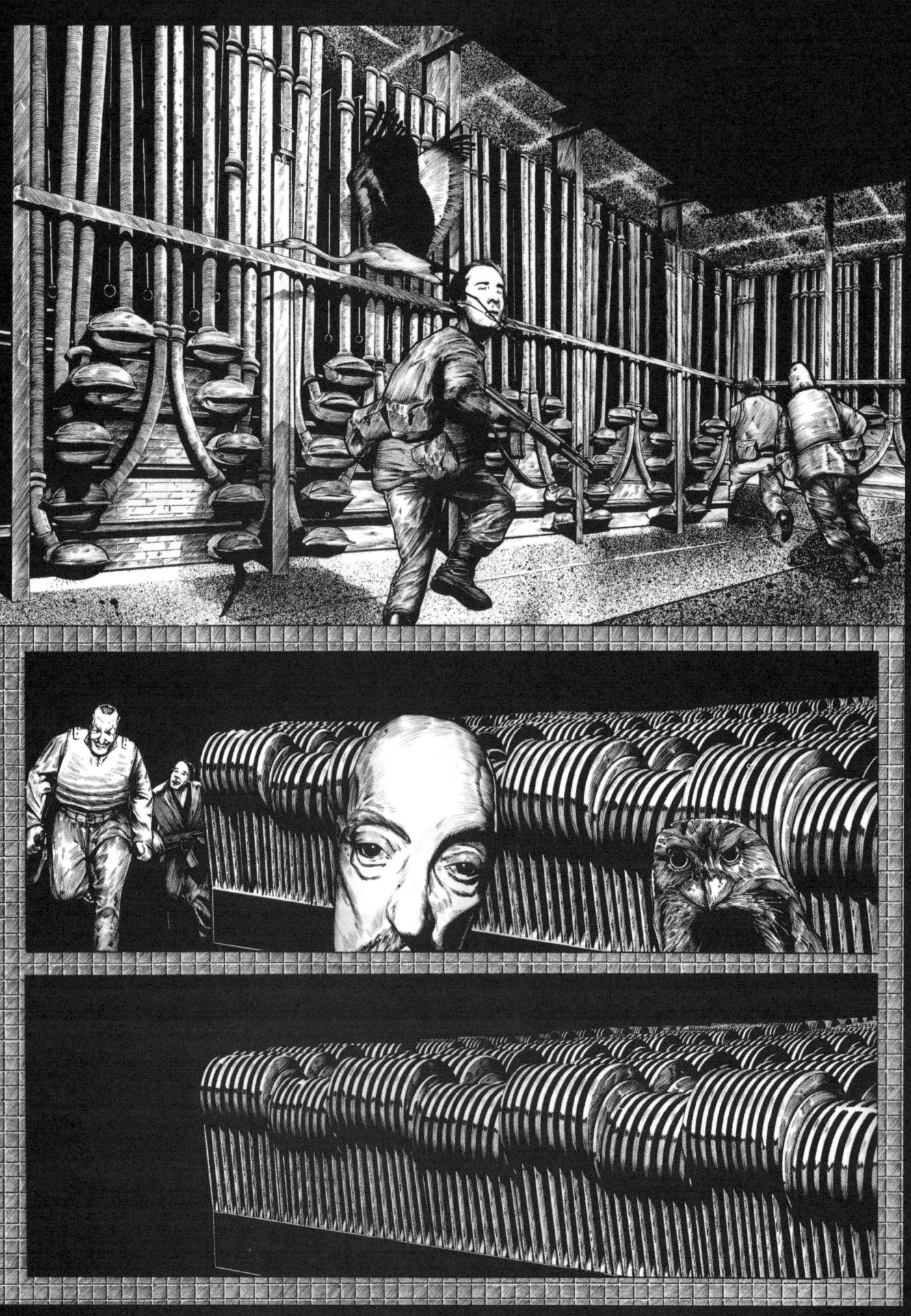
They are close now, I can smell them—fear, excitement, but most of all blood—the smell of elimination.

Silence. I know how the Registry operates. In my time with the Registry we never lost an individual listed in a warrant—no one has ever escaped.

The rush has gone and the aftertaste is kicking in. Time to think. Why? Why me? And why now? I have done the same as these people for most of my life. What has caused this change, what is different today from yesterday, hunter to hunted?

I say most of my life, but there was a time before the Registry—a lonely parentless boy in a series of grey-walled institutions. The Registry knows exactly where to find suitable employees—the alienated, disaffected, and dehumanized need little training and next to no motivation to do The Work.

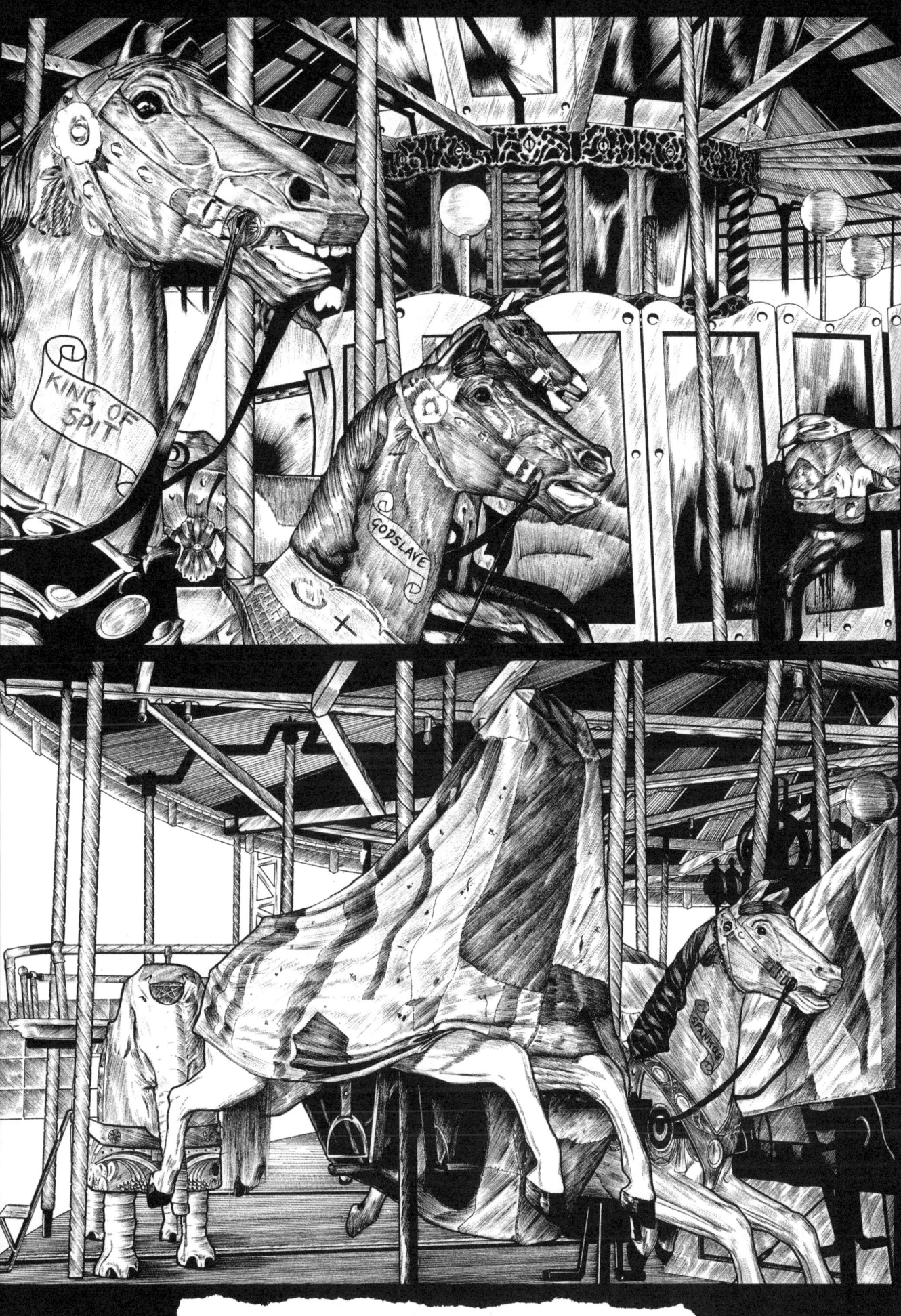

My childhood memories have been altered by my present circumstances. What happy times there were have vanished, replaced by brutality and fear.

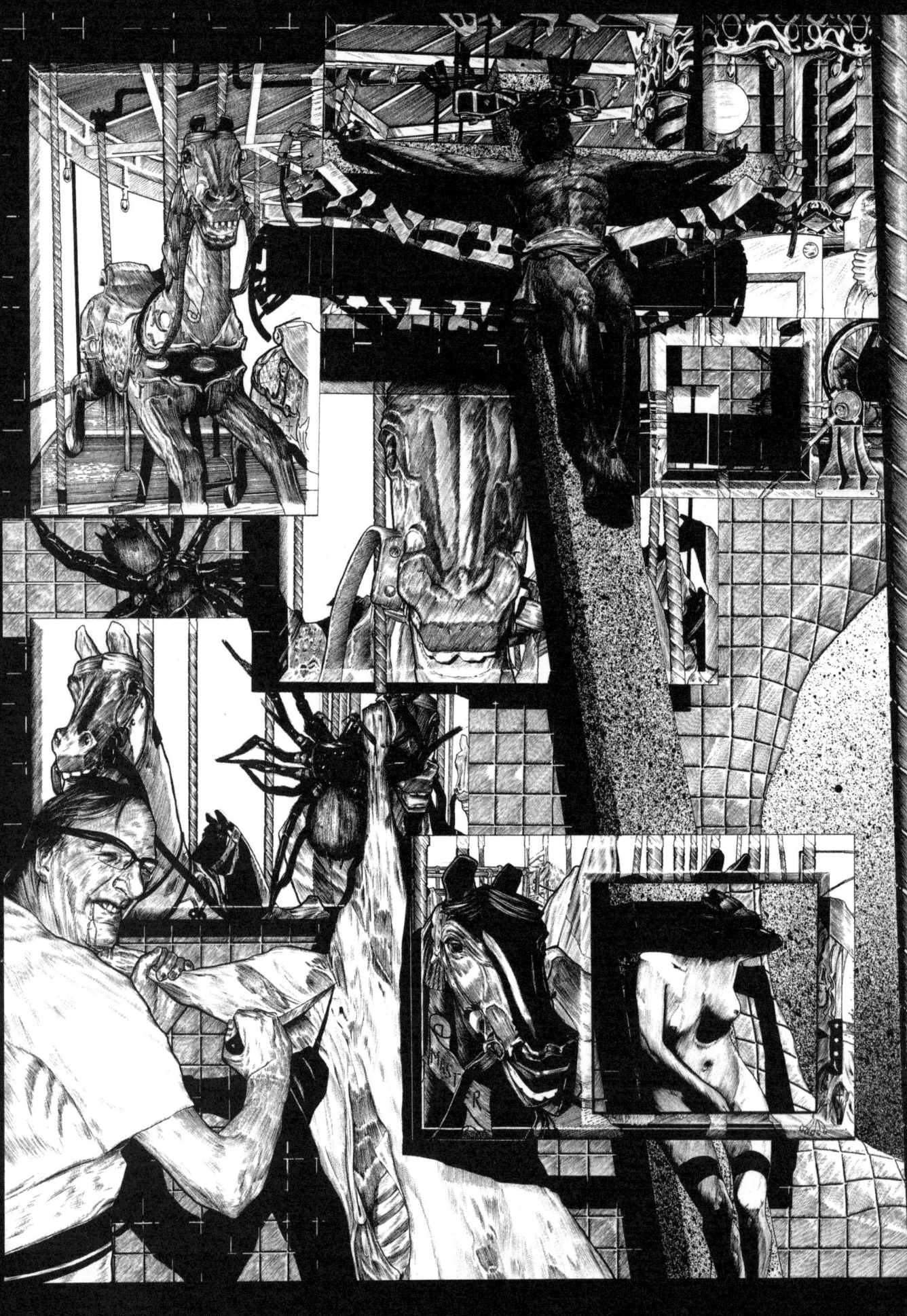

Surrounded again by familiar images of slaughter, I know I have returned. The immediate threat is dead but they will send more . . . we always do.

Why? The question pumps relentlessly through my head. What have I done to change things? The bodies that surround me used to be my co-workers. One had even been a friend, as much as anyone in the Registry ever can be. I had been forced to eliminate them. It makes no sense.

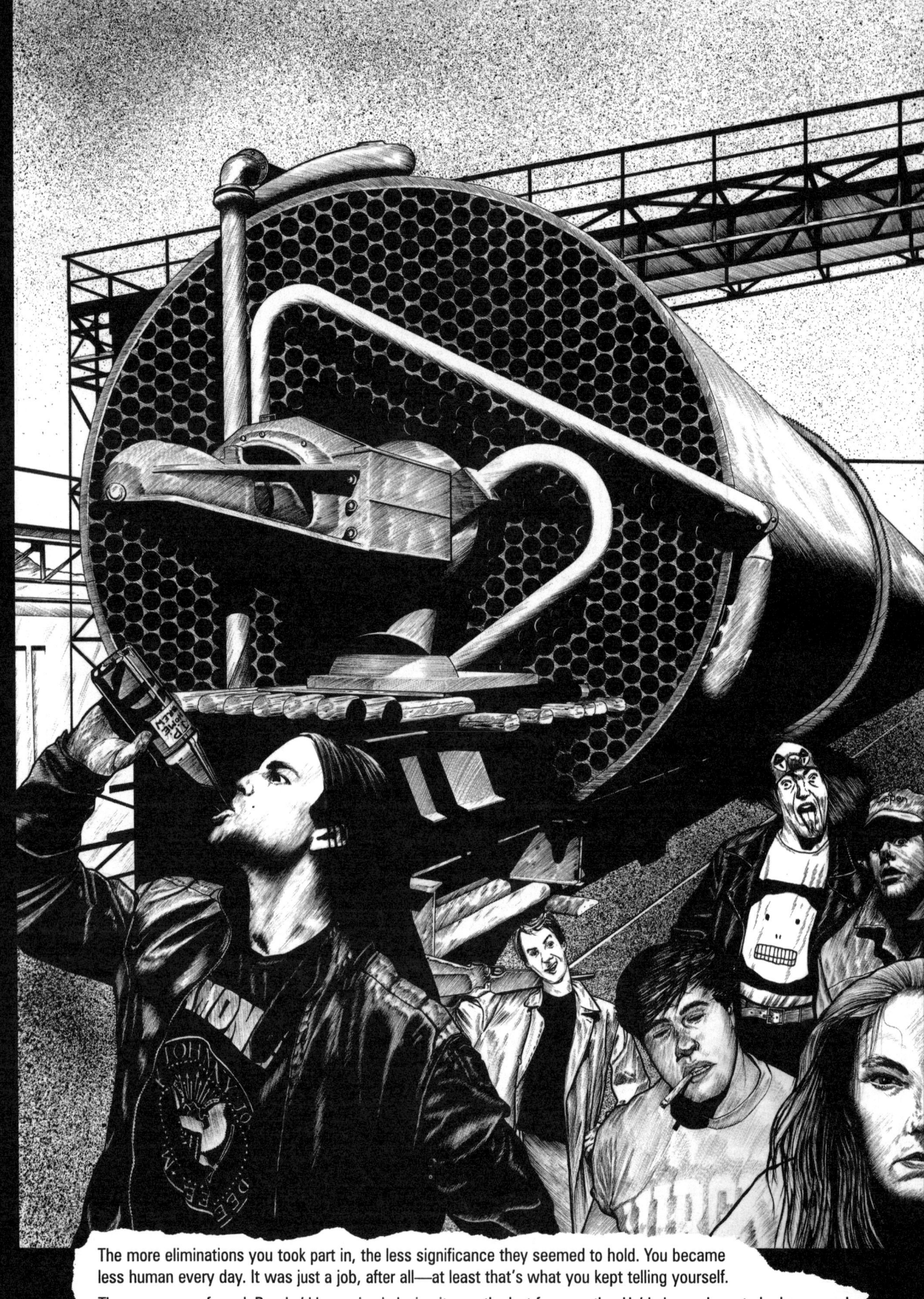

The more eliminations you took part in, the less significance they seemed to hold. You became less human every day. It was just a job, after all—at least that's what you kept telling yourself.

There was one of us, J. P., who'd been slowly losing it over the last few months. He'd always have to be hammered during an elimination, just so that things would work. The last one we did was less than two weeks ago.

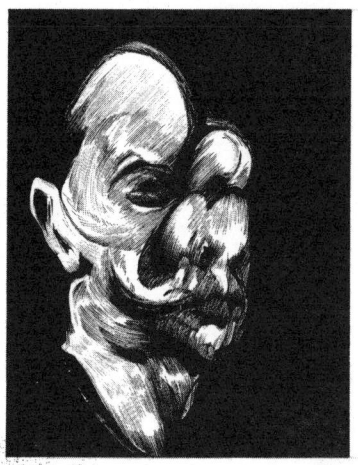 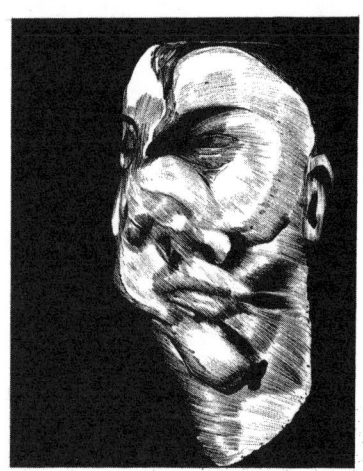

It was just another run-of-the-mill family elimination. As with most eliminations it involved surprise.

Just as with most eliminations it involved a large, brutal group of Registry officers.

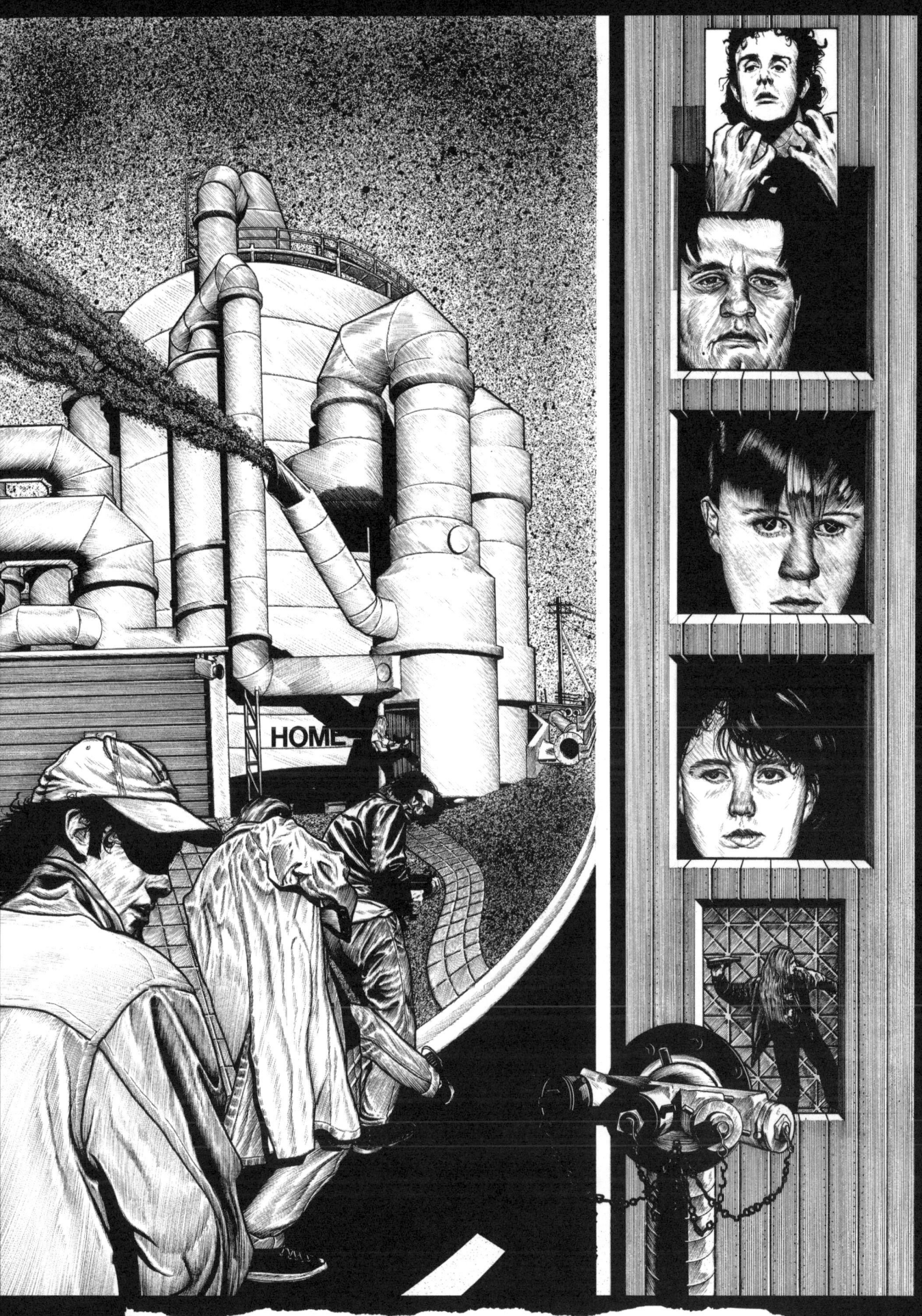

What J. P. was finding increasingly difficult was that all eliminations involve death. I could see it in his face, and I can remember thinking at the time that I was beginning to understand him.

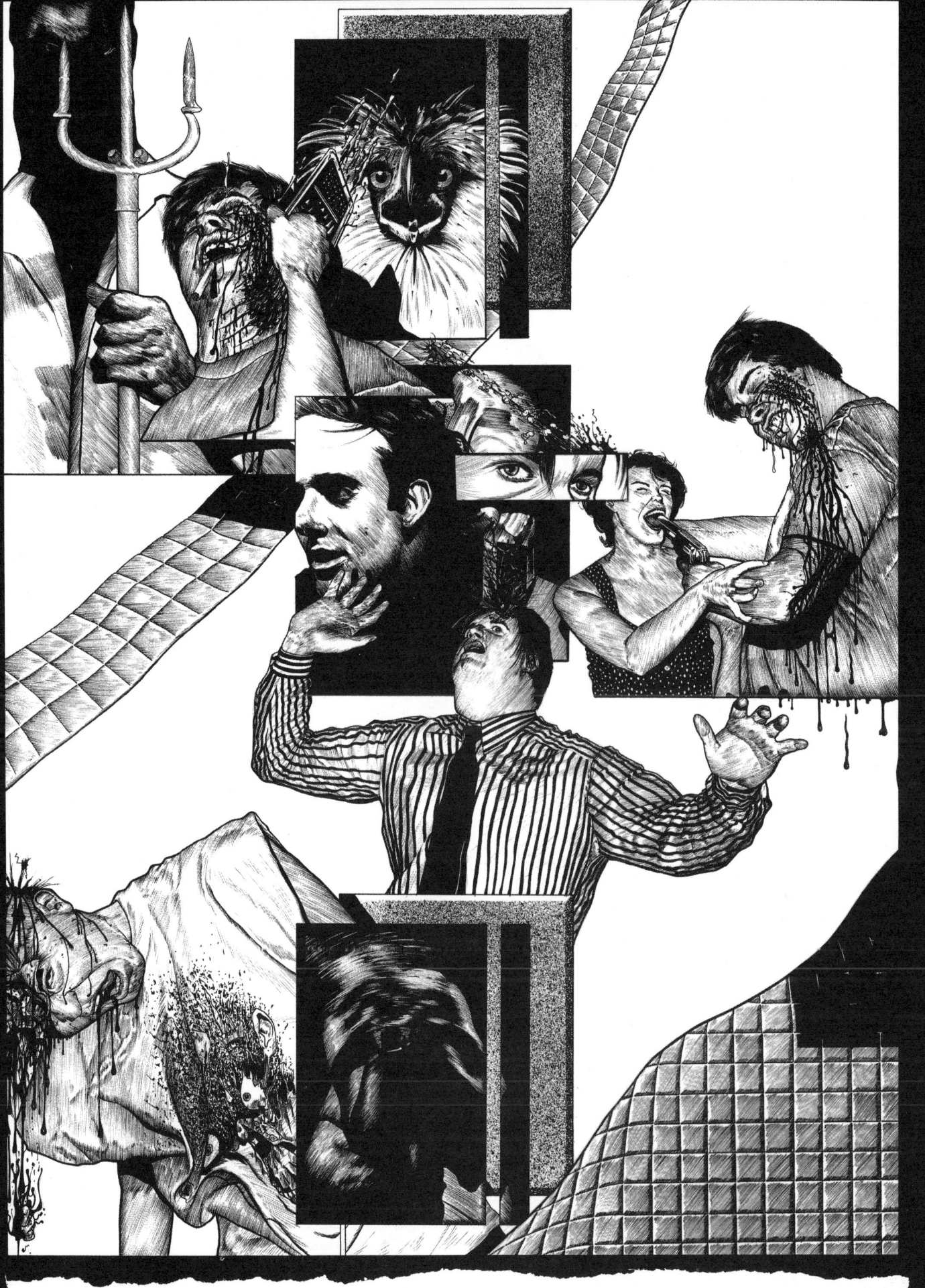

My memories of these events are clearer than anything else. The eliminations always remain, no matter how many or how brutal.

In that spacious, comfortable office on the top floor of the Registry building, new orders will be given. They will be sent on their way to eliminate me.

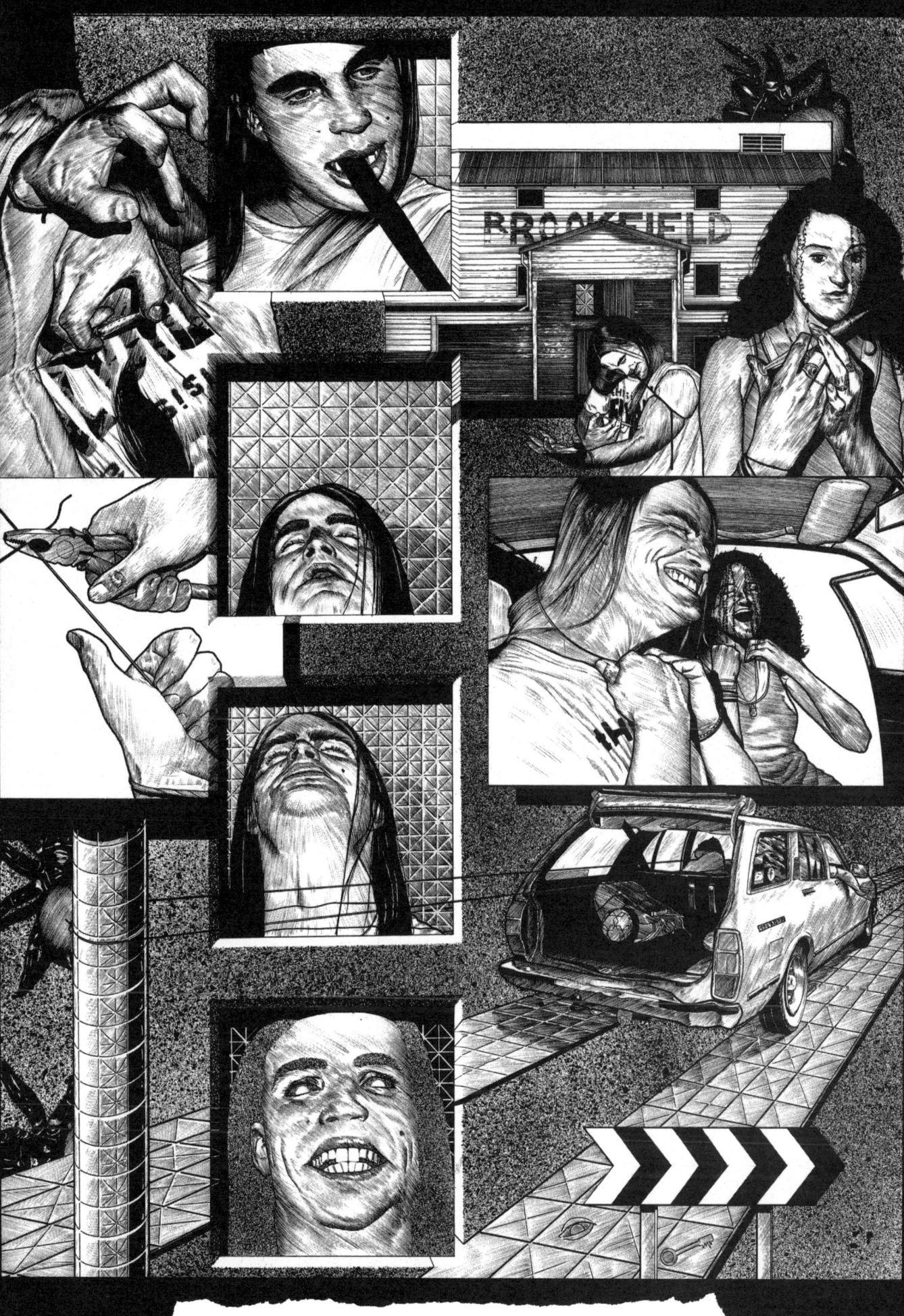

I think J. P. knew something that he shouldn't—the truth—or at least a clearer version of it—for truth has degrees just like everything else in this place.

Shortly after we'd spoken, J. P. and his girlfriend ended it all in typically brutal fashion. The Registry wrote his death off as a result of work-related stress, not an uncommon end for Registry people. At the time I couldn't help thinking there was something very strange about this one. Now I'm positive.

They are here as I knew they would be. There will be more than last time. I will know them all, to varying degrees, just as they know me.

Waiting, knowing.

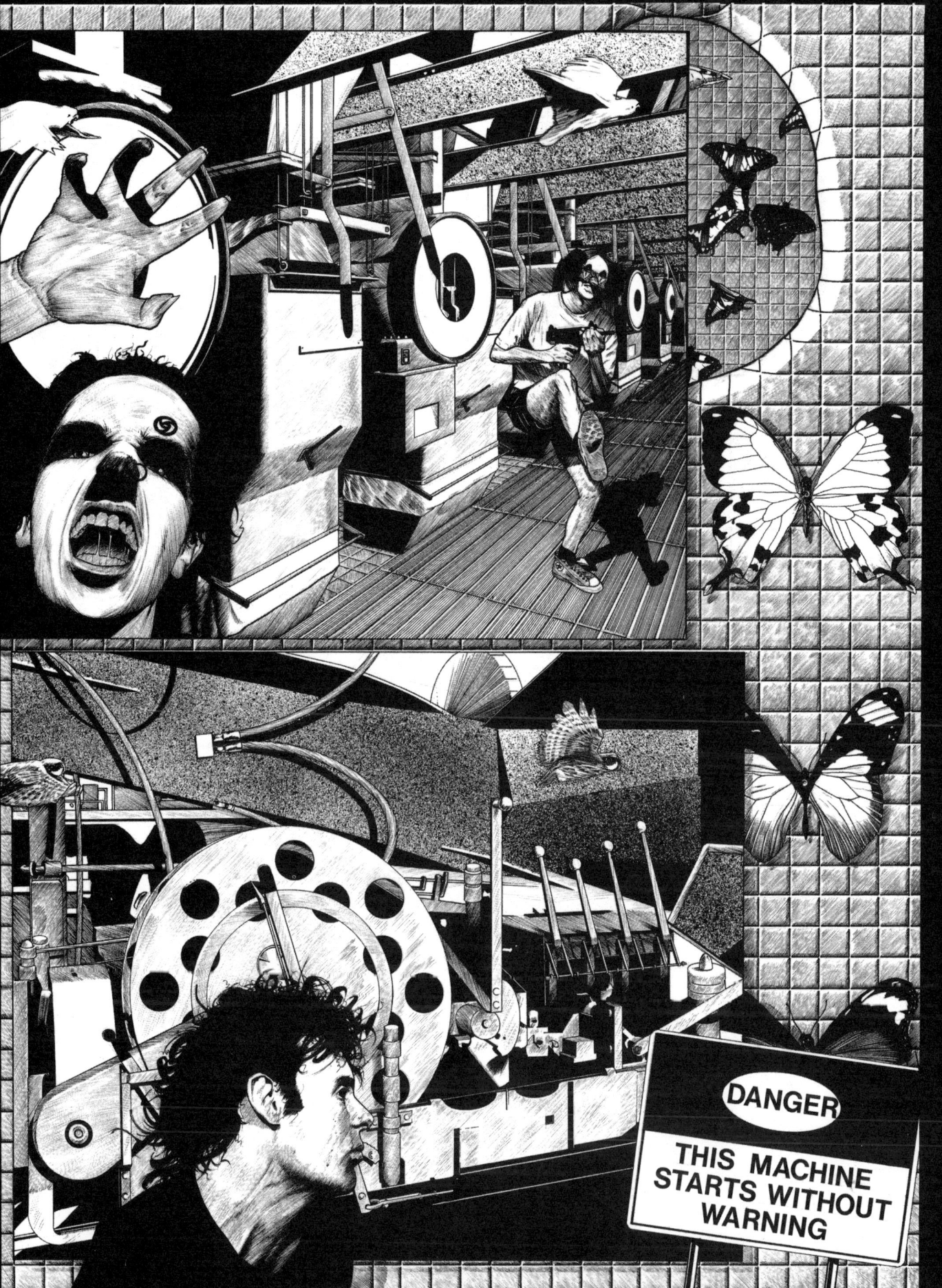

Seconds pass. My fear evaporates into pure adrenaline as the games begin—I will make them work for this elimination bonus.

The boys lose. My head fills with clichés—survival of the fittest, meanest, crazed, lost. Now for the old man.

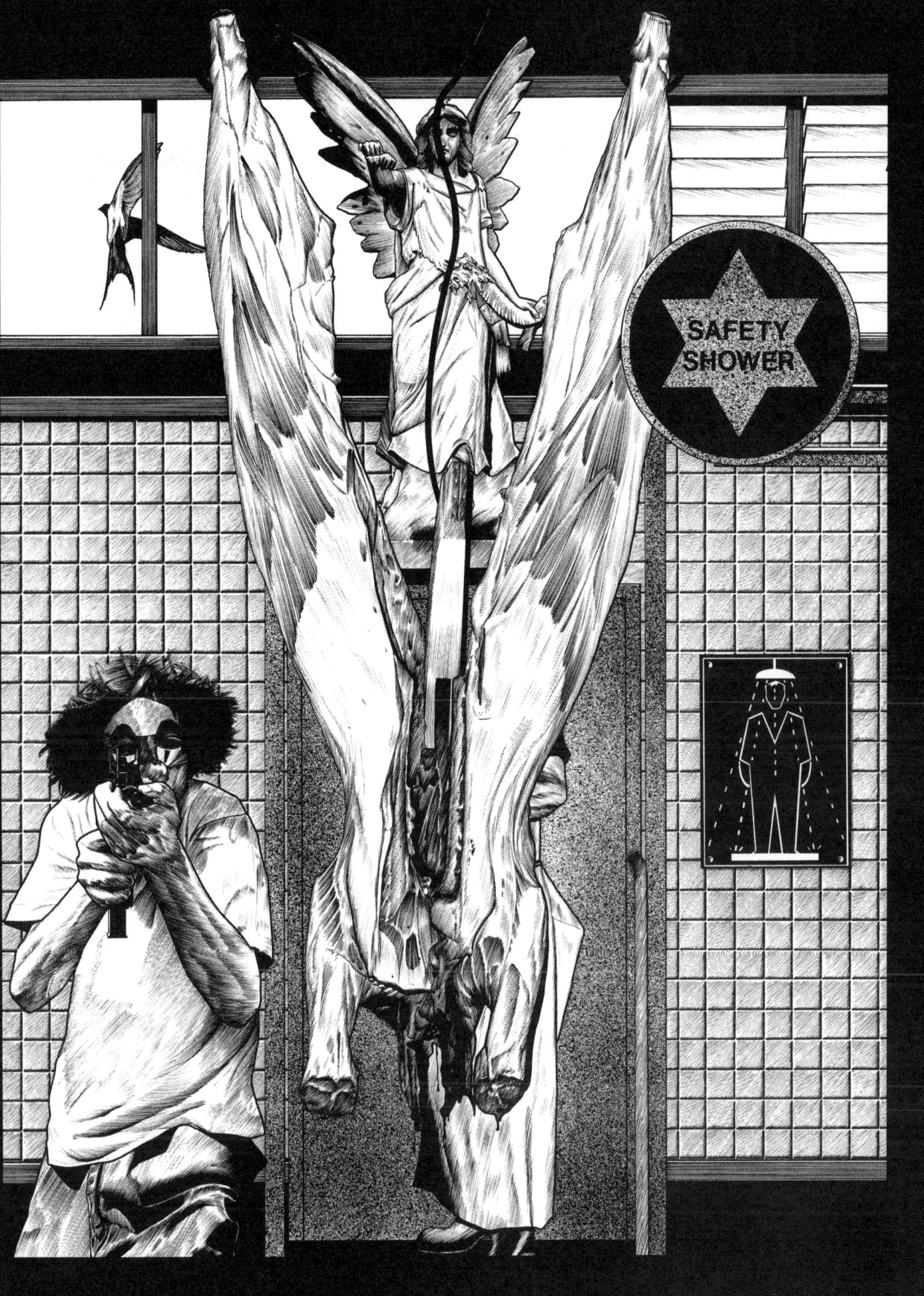

Familiar surroundings rush past. I am more at home now; this feels good.

They have chosen well. This a place of sanctuary, but not a place to die—at least not for me.

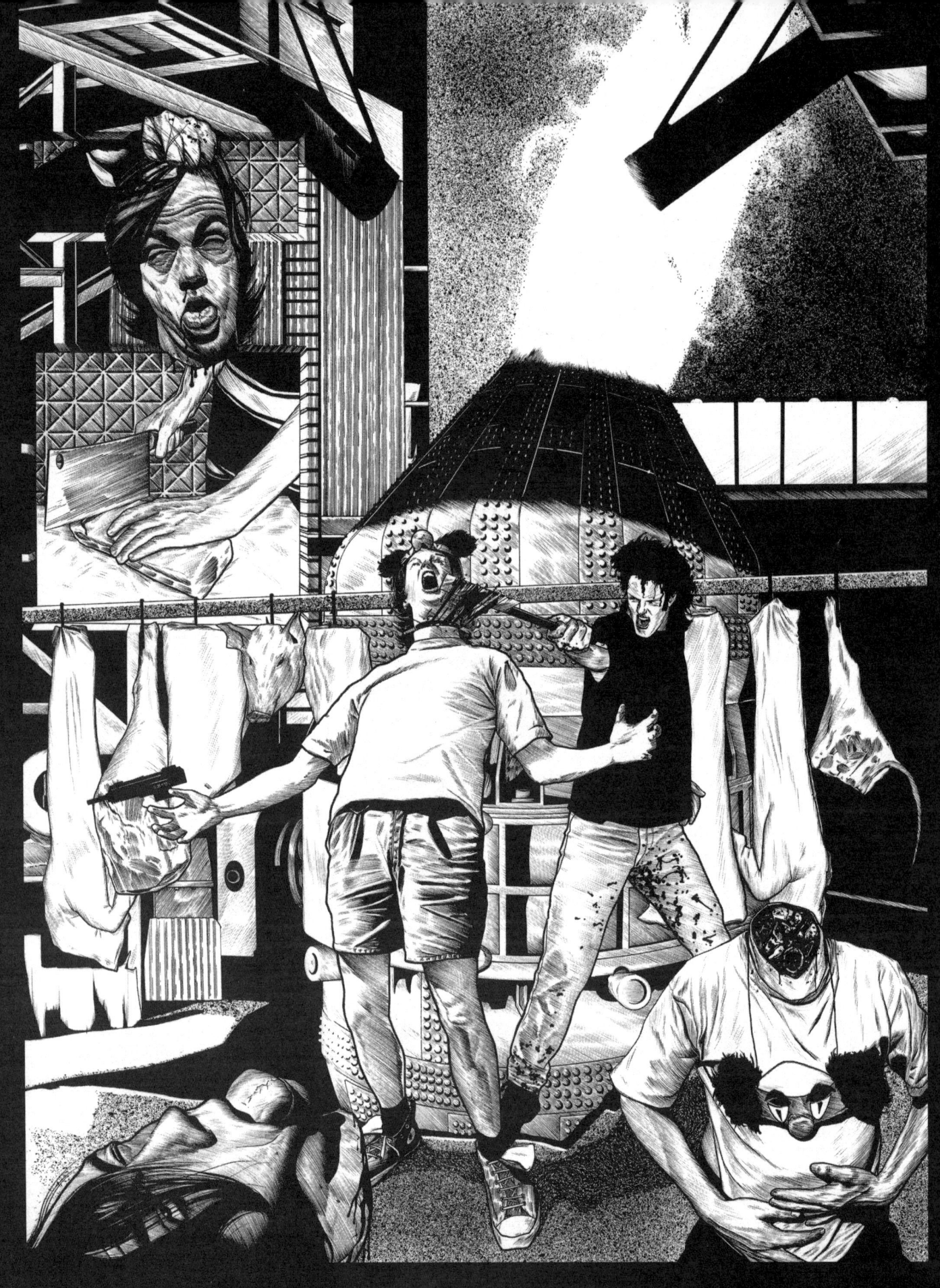
"A clean sharp blade chops better."

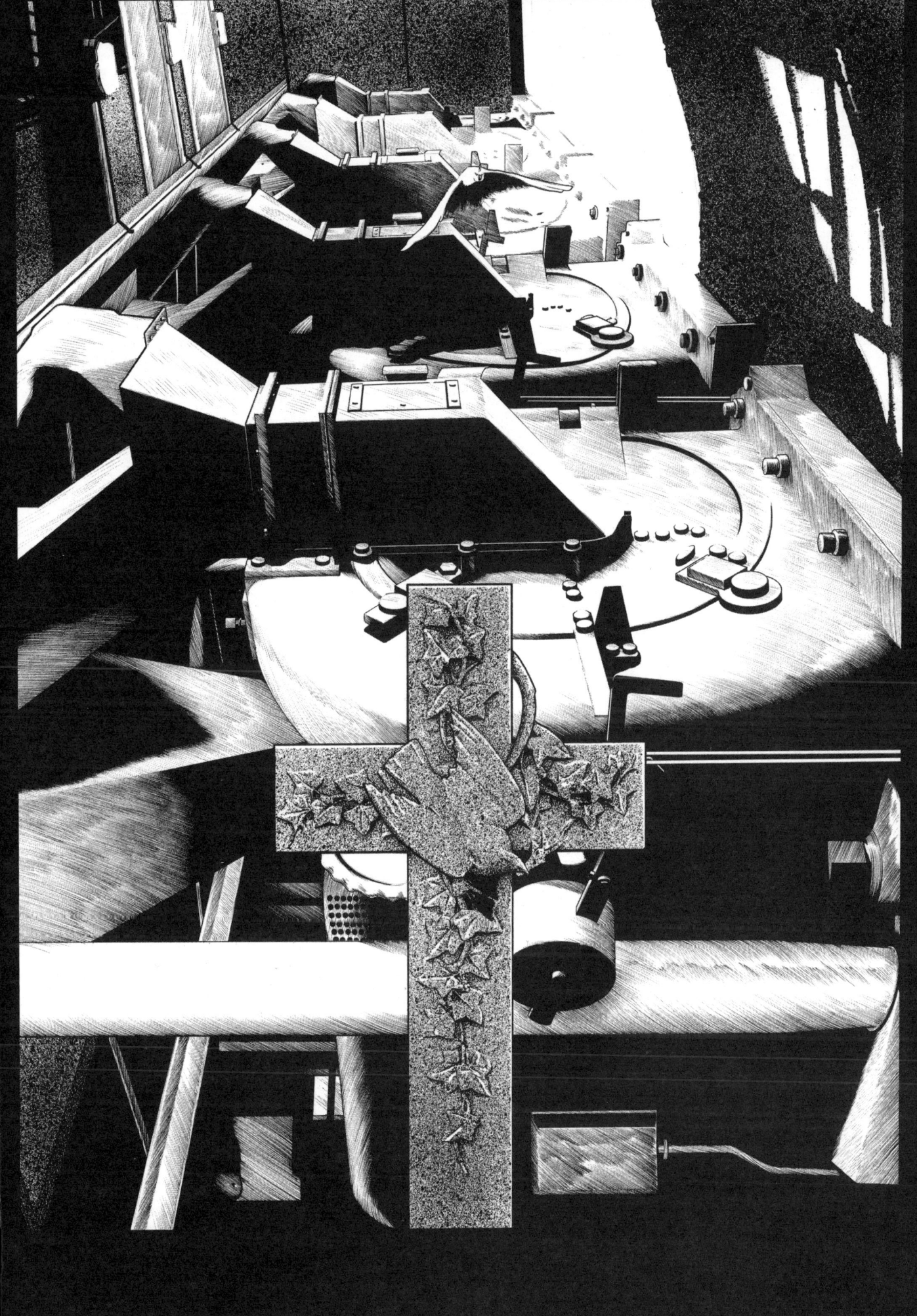

Time to think. Time to stop. Thoughts and images crowd my head. A path emerges slowly. It's familiar, overgrown and inviting.

The further I go along this path, the deeper I seem to be going into my past. Memories are sifting through my mind—an answer seems to be forming, but I can't quite grasp it yet.

I am being drawn deeper. A childhood forgotten and lost—an adolescence—covered in blood and guts. There is an answer here somewhere—I can really feel it now, brooding, forming, escaping.

My head feels fit to explode, there can be no other explanation. No other reason.

I'm short of breath. It is here. I grew up an orphan, and I will die an orphan. The last job I did was a routine elimination of a forty-eight-year-old woman—I now know that the illegal must be my mother. It all makes perfect sense. J. P. was right. I have killed my own mother. They used me to kill my own mother. I'm dead now.

Section 27; *Following the successful Registry-certified elimination of an individual, all biological issue of that individual will be subsequently listed for elimination.*

If I had known, nothing would've been different. We'd both still be dead—but at least I would not have pulled the trigger, and at least my mother would not have died at the hands of her own son.

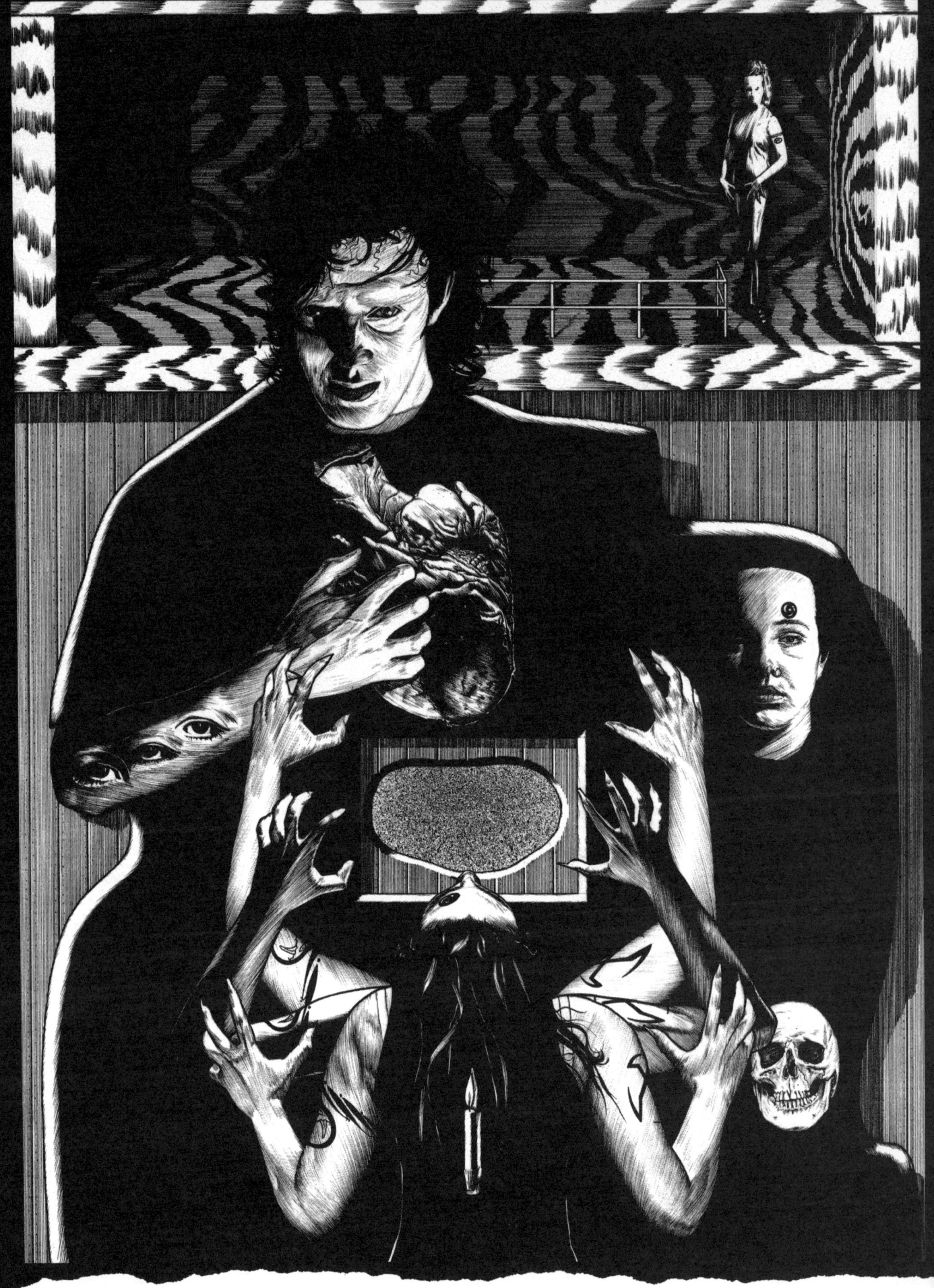
A kind of reckless sleep catches my breath and my head pounds uncontrollably—death surrounds, invading, intrusive, well within reach.

Instinct drives me to keep moving but I see little point now. Running, panting, sweating, from one death comes another.

Is that it?

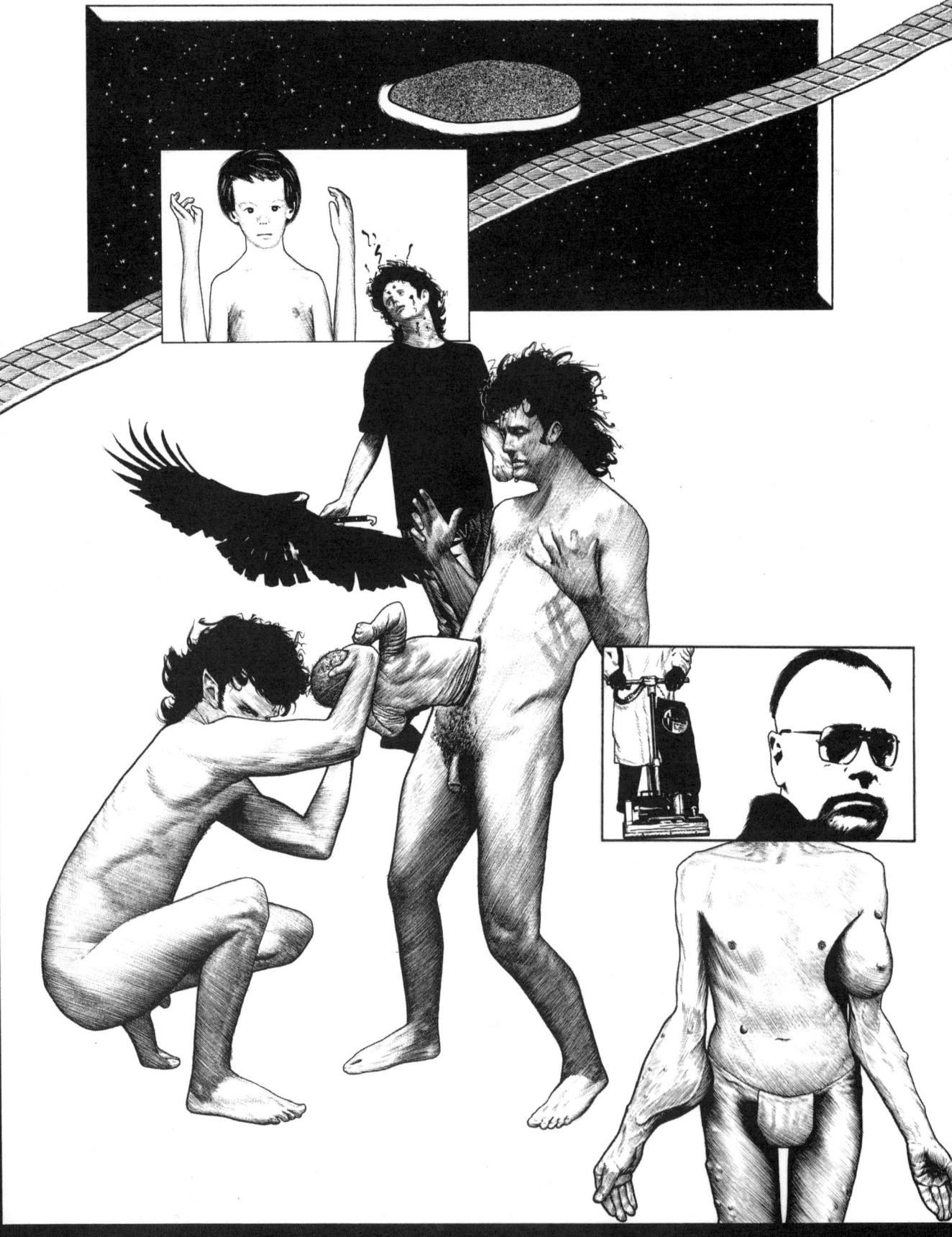

In the end it didn't matter who, or how, or where—in fact, none of the details mattered, just the fact itself. That fact alone was enough to explain all that had gone before and all that was to come. My part in everything was meaningless save that I served to occupy space and time and to keep the Registry busy. My mother had kept the Registry busy. They had spent my life trying to find her, and when they did they sent me to eliminate her. She did not recognize me, and I did not recognize her.
The Registry will always be busy.

Matt Coyle lives in Sydney, Australia. He completed two years of art school before beginning work on *Registry of Death*. This, his first published work, took him two years to complete. On the rare occasions when he isn't drawing, Matt works as a wardsman in various hospitals in Sydney.

Peter Lamb was born in Canberra, Australia in 1972. He wrote *Registry of Death* whilst completing his honors degree in philosophy. The subject matter strongly reflects his interests in the harsh realities of the human condition and the unceasing search for reason in what appears to be an entirely unreasonable world.